# Ponko

and the

## South Pole

Dedicated to Will and Mike Cross and their journey
to the South Pole to raise funds for diabetes research.

A percentage of the author's proceeds from this book
will go to the Juvenile Diabetes Research Foundation.
www.jdf.org
www.curewalk.com

First published in Great Britain in 2002 by
Frances Lincoln Limited, 4 Torriano Mews,
Torriano Avenue, London NW5 2RZ
www.franceslincoln.com

British Library Cataloguing in Publication Data available on request

ISBN 0-7112-1942-7

Printed in Singapore
1 3 5 7 9 8 6 4 2

# Ponko
## and the
## South Pole

MEREDITH HOOPER

*Illustrated by* JAN ORMEROD

In association with
the National Maritime Museum,
Greenwich, London

FRANCES LINCOLN

One night on the edge of Antarctica, Ponko the Penguin sat down to a special feast. Next to him was a small bear with a long, woolly scarf.

"There aren't any bears in Antarctica," said Ponko.
"There are now," said the bear. "There's me. Joey Bear."

"Do you know when they're leaving?" asked Joey Bear, pointing to the explorers who were singing loud songs at the other end of the hut. "I don't want to miss the Great Expedition to the South Pole."

"Nor me either," said Ponko, wondering what kind of a pole the South Pole was.

The explorers were definitely getting ready.
Sleeping bags and tents and boxes of food
were piled on to the sledges.

Ponko and Joey scrambled up on to the last sledge.
They were just in time. Everyone gave three cheers,
and the Great Expedition to the South Pole set off.

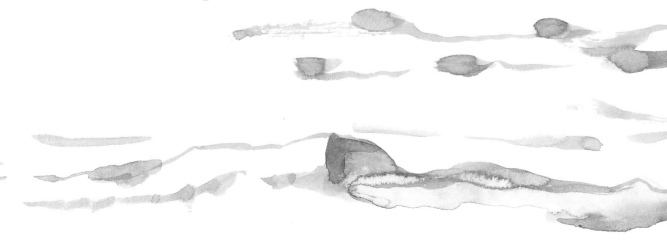

When night came, the explorers put up their tents.
Ponko discovered a useful supply of square expedition
biscuits. Joey found a huge bag of chocolate raisins.

# AAARK! AAARK!

A line of penguins shuffled past.
They stared at Ponko and Joey.

"Where are you going?" they demanded.
"To the South Pole," said Ponko proudly.
"Oh no you're not," said the penguins.
"No one goes to the South Pole."

"Well we are," said Ponko.

But he wished he knew where
the South Pole was.

At the end of the next day, Ponko and Joey
lay on their sledge gazing up at the silent moon.

# HARRUMPH!

A silvery seal slithered past.

"Where are you two going?"
asked the seal.

"To the South Pole," said Ponko firmly.

"Oh dear oh dear," said the seal.
"The South Pole is far away and high up,
in the Great White Emptiness. I'd turn
around and go home if I were you."

In the morning, as Ponko and Joey were riding along,
suddenly . . .

# CRASH!

their sledge was falling,

then

# BUMP!

it stopped with a terrible jerk.

Ponko and Joey were down inside the ice.
Far above they could see a patch of sky.
Below was empty darkness.

But before they knew it, the explorers
were pulling on ropes, and their sledge
began heaving

up, up

between the blue ice walls.

"Hang on tight!" whispered Ponko.

It was wonderful being back in the sunshine.
Joey held on to Ponko's flippers.
   "I'm glad we've got each other," he said.

But then a dreadful thing happened. Ponko and Joey
fell off the sledge. Nobody noticed that they were gone.

One moment they were there, rushing along.
The next they were lying in the snow, left behind.

The noises of the Great Expedition to the South Pole
faded into the distance. Ponko and Joey lay in the snow,
and a profound silence settled around them.

So this is the end of our Great Expedition, thought Ponko, sadly.
We shall just lie here on the way to the South Pole.
Tears welled into his eyes, and froze.

# SWOOSH!

A big, bold bird landed on the snow.
  "You don't belong here," said the bird.
"And you aren't even worth eating.
Explain yourselves."

"We were hoping to go to the South Pole,"
said Ponko, but his voice came out all squeaky,
by mistake.

"Is that your problem!" cackled the bird. "I can
take you, if you like. Sid Skua at your service!"

"How do you know the way?" asked Ponko.
"It's easy," said Sid. "I just keep flying south.
When I can't go any further south,
I've arrived."

"Oh," said Ponko. "I see."
But he didn't really.

Sid hovered, picked Ponko and Joey up,
and began flying with slow beats of his strong wings.

They flew over icy glaciers all crumpled and frozen.

They flew past mountains with rocky peaks
jutting up like sharp teeth.

Then they were flying over the Great White Emptiness.

Nothing moved on it. Only their shadows.

At last they landed.

"This is it," said Sid. "This is the South Pole."

Excitedly Ponko and Joey looked around.
Snow and ice, ice and snow, stretched in all directions.
The wind blew freezing cold.

"I can't see a pole anywhere," said Ponko, very puzzled.

Sid cackled. "You can't see one because there isn't one! The South Pole is only a place. Not a thing."

So this is what exploring is all about, thought Ponko. How far away it felt from everywhere else. He wished he could leave a flag, or a tin with a message, to show that they had been here.

Then Ponko had an idea. He stood very straight and said in a loud voice,

"Joey and I declare that we are the first to reach the South Pole."

"Don't be so silly," screeched Sid. "What about me? What about all my mates?"

"Of course," said Ponko humbly. "I'm sorry."

Then Ponko had another idea. He stood very tall and said,

"I declare that I am the first Penguin to reach the South Pole."
"And I," said Joey, "am the first Bear."

Then Ponko and Joey did a small happy dance in the snow, to celebrate.

"Time to go," said Sid. "It's far too cold to stay."

He picked up Ponko and Joey, and with slow beats
of his strong wings headed north.

They flew across the Great White Emptiness,
back over the mountains and glaciers,
on and on over snow and ice, ice and snow.

At last Sid turned and swooped down.
There, like a box on the edge of the ice-filled ocean,
was the expedition hut.

Sid sat Ponko and Joey on an upturned sledge.
   "That will surprise those explorers!" he cackled, and flew off.

Joey leaned against Ponko, almost asleep. Ponko felt very tired.
And hungry. But most of all he felt very happy.

He and Joey Bear had been all the way to the South Pole.

And all the way back again.

Ponko the Penguin belonged to the photographer Herbert Ponting
who went to Antarctica with the explorer Captain Scott
on an expedition around 100 years ago.
This is a photograph of Ponko who can be seen
at the National Maritime Museum in Greenwich, London.
www.nmm.ac.uk

Joey Bear is based on the bear who went to Antarctica
with the scientist Frank Debenham on the same expedition.
This photograph of the bear was taken by Herbert Ponting.